Nick, mandy Luond

COME HERE, LITTLE HEDGEHOG

Original edition published in German by Franz Schneider Verlag,
GmbH, West Germany

© 1987 by Franz Schneider Verlag GmbH

Translation copyright © 1988 by Abingdon Press

Library of Congress Cataloging-in-Publication Data

Michels, Tilde.
  [Igel, komm, ich nehm dich mit. English]
  Come here, little hedghog / Tilde Michels : illustrations by Sara
Ball ; translated by Anna Lass-Potter.
    p. cm.
  Summary: A little girl finds a hedgehog in the garden and decides
to keep him as a pet but can't understand why he doesn't seem happy.
  Translation of: Igel, komm, ich nehm dich mit.
  ISBN 0-687-08876-3 (alk. paper)
  1. Hedgehogs—Juvenile fiction.   [1. Hedghogs—Fiction.
2. Pets—Fiction.] I. Ball, Sara. ill. II. Title.
PZ10.3.M5773Co 1988
[E]—dc19
                88-16600
                CIP
                AC

ISBN 0-687-08876-3

This book is printed on acid-free paper.

Printed in Singapore

Come Here, Little Hedgehog

Tilde Michels

illustrations by **Sara Ball**

translated by Anna Lass-Potter

ABINGDON PRESS / Nashville

The sun slips behind the clouds and twilight spreads over the sky. It is just the right time for hedgehogs to search for snails and to look for their friends.

One little hedgehog crawls out from his sleeping place and sniffs the evening air. Then he runs over the meadow and along the garden fence.

There Lee Anna discovers him.
"Don't roll into a ball, little hedgehog,"
she says. "Please don't be frightened.
Come home with me. I'll be good to you."

The hedgehog's spines are sharp, so Lee Anna spreads her jacket over him and wraps him up in it.

Through the jacket she can feel his little heart beating fast. She says to herself, "I can tame him and he will stay with me forever. He will be a good pet."

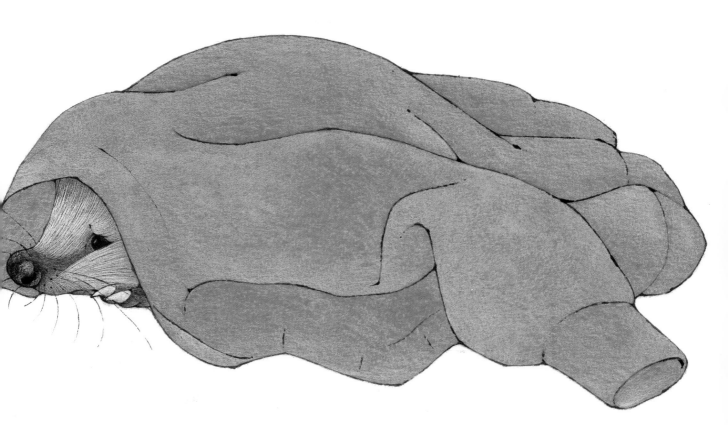

At home Lee Anna carries a cage into her room. She covers the floor of the cage with straw and puts the hedgehog down into it. Then night comes.

"You must go to sleep now, my little pet," Lee Anna says. But the hedgehog does not want to sleep. He is used to roaming at night.

Lee Anna hears him rustling in the straw. She hears him gnawing at the bars as he tries to break out of the cage.

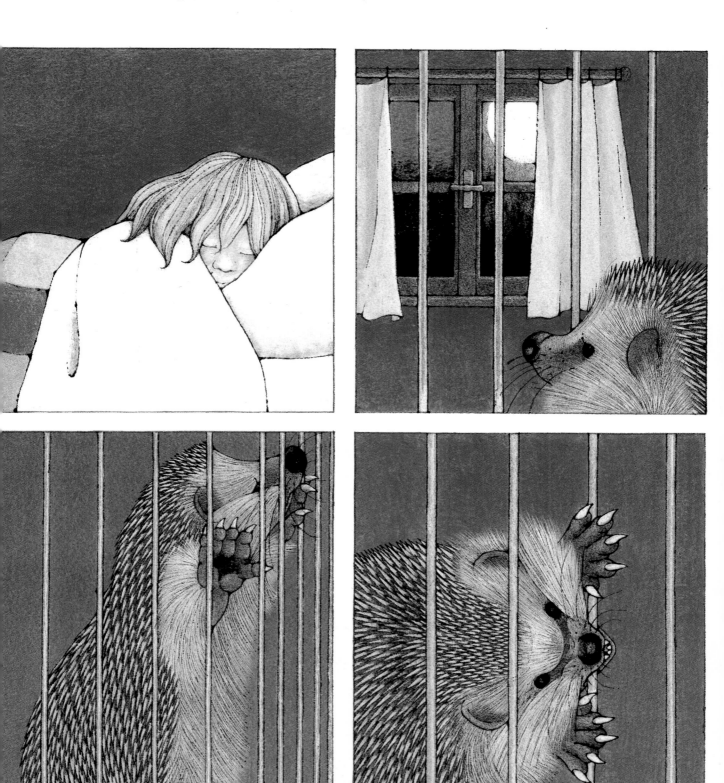

The next morning Lee Anna's mother says, "A hedgehog doesn't like to be caged. See how sad he looks. I think you should set him free again."

"He will be better soon," Lee Anna answers, "because I love him so much!"

But things do not get better. Every night the little hedgehog wanders around in his cage close to the bars. Every day he lies rolled up in one corner. Sometimes Lee Anna can even hear him sigh.

"What's wrong with him?" she asks. "I give him egg yolk and hamburger meat and everything else a hedgehog needs."

"You have to set him free," her mother says again.

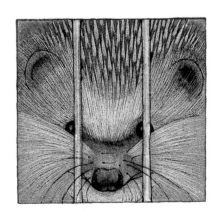

Lee Anna runs to find her grandpa.

"I want to keep my little hedgehog! I love him so much, Grandpa. Do you think he doesn't like me?"

Grandpa thinks a while, then says, "Let me tell you a story."

He takes her on his lap and begins. "Once upon a time there was a little girl called Lee Anna."

"Me?" asks Lee Anna.

"It is only a story," Grandpa says with a smile. "Lee Anna was a very happy little girl who loved to run and play in the meadow.

"One day as Lee Anna was playing with her ball in the grass, she saw something very big in front of her.

"It was a gigantic hedgehog with huge paws. He stooped down to Lee Anna and said, 'I like you, little girl. I'll take you home with me to my family. You'll like living with us.'

"Lee Anna did not understand the hedgehog's language. She only saw that the hedgehog wanted to grab her.

"And she ran away.

"But the hedgehog caught up with her. 'Don't be afraid,' he said, 'I won't hurt you.'

"He took her in his paws and picked her up. Very tenderly and carefully, he carried her to his burrow. There he put her into a cage so she couldn't run away.

"All the hedgehog family liked the cute little girl. Everybody wanted to pet her. But Lee Anna was afraid of their claws. She was afraid when they leaned over the cage, looked at her, and grunted. And she did not want to be locked in.

"The hedgehogs gave Lee Anna a soft bed of straw and they were very good to her.

"But everything was so different in their home.

"At night, when Lee Anna wanted to sleep, the hedgehogs were wide awake and noisy.

"In the morning, when Lee Anna woke up and wanted to play, the hedgehogs snuggled up with each other and slept.

"Lee Anna felt terribly strange and lonely with them. 'I don't fit in with you,' she sobbed. 'I want to go home.'

"But the hedgehogs didn't understand her, and Lee Anna grew more and more unhappy each day."

Grandpa pauses for a minute.

Lee Anna looks at him with big eyes. "How does the story end?" she asks.

"I don't know," Grandpa says and gives her a big hug.

Suddenly Lee Anna realizes how the story should end.

When she takes the hedgehog out to the meadow, she is still a little sad. Then she watches how he lifts his little nose, how he sniffs the open air.

"Well, Grandpa," Lee Anna says, "he is happy again now, isn't he?" And then she adds, "If I put out something for him to eat one evening . . . maybe he'll come back and visit me."